THE GREEDY CAKE LION

Look out for this slice of cake as you read the story.

Roary the lion has a sweet tooth.
Or rather, sweet jaws!
But he is VERY fussy, so
everything has to be just right.
Otherwise he kicks up a BIG fuss!

I only eat
the best cake.

Fussy Roary loves to eat his cakes at home. That way, he can be sure he's eating the best possible cake!

Thank you, Sir!
11 12 1 2 3 4 5 6 7 8 9 10

But when Roary visits Giraffe and eats his eclairs he finds them too creamy. He still gobbles them up though!

Ugh, far too creamy. How disgusting.
Hmph!

He finds the meerkat's cupcakes far too sweet but he still eats them all up.

Unbelievable!

Crocodile's chocolate cake is too dry, but
Roary swallows a whole cake in one big bite.

He's so rude!
Why did he eat it?

Zebra's doughnuts aren't exciting enough, but that doesn't stop Roary from munching them all down.

MUNCH!
MUNCH!
So, dull.
Sir, don't be
so unkind!

The other animals have had enough. Roary has complained too much about their cakes and they are fed up.

But what can they do?

The animals have decided, there will be no more sweet treats for Roary. They have had enough!

How can Roary make it up to them?

Roary's Roarsome
Bakery

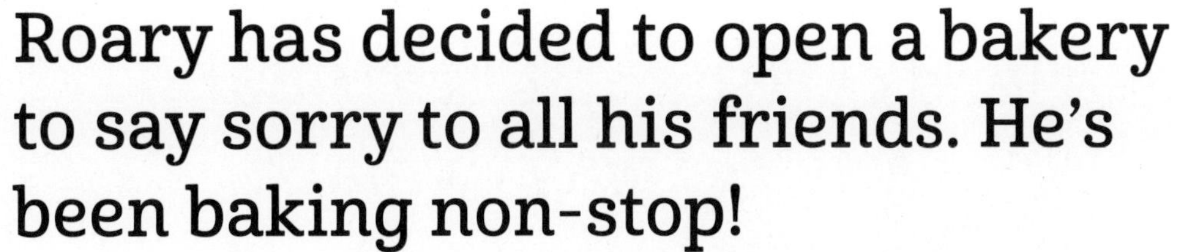

Roary has decided to open a bakery to say sorry to all his friends. He's been baking non-stop!

But will anyone come to taste his yummy cakes?

The bakery is open and all of Roary's friends are here to try it out. What a sweet way to make it up to them!
Ooh, Yum!

oary's Roarsome
Bakery
I'm sorry my dear friends.
Free cakes for everyone!

Everyone loves Roary's cakes. They're not too dry, too creamy, too dull or too sweet!

Well done, Sir!

The Greedy Cake Lion

A LAUGHING LOBSTER BOOK 978-1-910764-64-0
Published in Great Britain by Laughing Lobster, an imprint of Centum Publishing Ltd.
This edition published 2022.

1 3 5 7 9 10 8 6 4 2

Illustrations by Sophie Hanton.

Laughing Lobster, an imprint of Centum Publishing Ltd, 20 Devon Square, Newton Abbot, Devon, TQ12 2HR, UK. Centum Publishing Ltd, 9/10 Fenian St, Dublin 2, D02 RX24, Ireland

books@centumpublishingltd.co.uk

LAUGHING LOBSTER, CENTUM PUBLISHING LIMITED Reg. No. 08497203

A CIP catalogue record for this book is available from the British Library.

Printed in China.